I am the WORST MOM

in the World Because . . .

Coreina Hubert

iUniverse books may be ordered through booksellers or by contacting:

iUniverse
1663 Liberty Drive
Bloomington, IN 47403
www.iuniverse.com
1-800-Authors (1-800-288-4677)

Because of the dynamic nature of the Internet, any web addresses or links contained in this book may have changed since publication and may no longer be valid. The views expressed in this work are solely those of the author and do not necessarily reflect the views of the publisher, and the publisher hereby disclaims any responsibility for them.

Any people depicted in stock imagery provided by Thinkstock are models, and such images are being used for illustrative purposes only.
Certain stock imagery © Thinkstock.

ISBN: 978-1-5320-4549-3 (sc)
ISBN: 978-1-5320-4551-6 (hc)
ISBN: 978-1-5320-4550-9 (e)

Print information available on the last page.

iUniverse rev. date: 03/24/2018

This book is dedicated for all those moms who put up with our whiny little kids, which eventually lead us to drinking more wine than we need to because of simple situations like these.

So please, fill up and take a sip when
you pass a familiar situation

I took my kids to the park, so I could drink coffee in peace

The kids didn't mind, but
the people walking
by the park did!

I made my toddler
wear a diaper
against his will

so he wouldn't poop
on the floor again.

I made my son
go back to bed

instead of allowing
him to watch TV at

3 AM in the morning.

I wouldn't let my
6 year old
Skip kindergarten today
Because
she was soooooo tired

So when I said
"no Netflix"......
she eventually
went to school.

Colouring is wonderful
Colouring is great

Colouring isn't needed
on the counter
When standing
at the bank

My toddler had
a tantrum

BECAUSE .....

I wouldn't allow her to
throw horse poop
at the cat.

I wouldn't allow
my 4 year old

**Wear a helmet
to DayCare.**

'14

Trips aren't
complete until
Someone forgets
something

And you
REFUSE TO TURN BACK
to get it.

As I kitchen multi-task,
my son asked me
for a sandwich.

I made him
ham and cheese
sandwich...

But instantly he protests
It isn't the right
sandwich!

Don't worry, I got it
right on the 3rd try..
the peanut butter
and jelly one.

Remember that sandwich
my son didn't want...
I ate it!

**Only to find out
seconds later
his sister wanted it.**

My toddler has a
thing for no clothes

I told him to
GO Get DRESSED

Results are astonishing.

Wearing one sock,
a pull up
and a hat.

After my toddler changed,

he than informed me
that he pooped
his pull ups

as he stuck his hands
inside of them...

I made him wash
his hands
and clean up.

I left my son crying
for 5 minutes
Behind a locked baby gate

as I finished painting
a piece of
Furniture.

The child being completely
traumatized from

me doing house work

Vs

attention to him

I won him back with Yogurt Tubes and Pepperoni.

I refused to give
my toddler
some of my Bagel..

He wants to eat
everything I eat

I usually hide food
behind my back or in
my shirt sleeve.

I told my 4 YR old to
GET OFF THE STAIRS

She told me "momma, I
am on the banister".

While waiting for the
car to get fixed

I played too hard
with my toddler.

Cooking a very
Healthy meal is almost
impossible
to get a toddler to eat

Especially when
dog food looks more
appetizing.

Ever try to fight with
A toddler over
BOOGERS

Right after wiping their nose?

Got the tears of madness
after
opening the banana

And breaking it
into two pieces.

Hand lotion seems to be a
hot in demand item today
and a "NO" for
consumption

Next is preventing
him from
licking it off the baby.

Today
I locked myself
In the bathroom

So I can eat a chocolate
bar in peace.

Everyone is soooo
needy,
Especially

when I am sick

Actually, you are the
Best mom in the
World, because
You too are
just like
the rest of us moms XO

And are not paying
attention to them as you
are reading this book.

Printed in the United States
By Bookmasters